I, CHARLES DARWIN

I, CHARLES DARWIN

*Being the Journal of His Visitation
to Earth in the Year 2009*

Nickell John Romjue

I, Charles Darwin: Being the Journal of His Visitation to Earth in the Year 2009

Published by Wheatmark®
610 Delano Street, Suite 104
Tucson, Arizona 85705, USA
www.wheatmark.com
Cover image of Charles Darwin courtesy corbinimages.com

Publisher's Cataloging-In-Publication Data
(Prepared by The Donohue Group, Inc.)

Romjue, Nickell John.
   I, Charles Darwin : being the journal of his visitation to Earth in the year 2009 / Nickell John Romjue. -- 1st ed.

      p. ; cm.

   Includes bibliographical references.
   ISBN: 978-1-60494-645-1

   1. Darwin, Charles, 1809–1882 — Influence — Fiction. 2. Science and civilization — Fiction. 3. Naturalism — Fiction. 4. Historical fiction. 5. Diary fiction. I. Title.

PS3618.O648 I35 2011
813/.6   2011930943

*To the passing of the great secular creed
that fatefully shaped the mind of the modern world,
and to the many millions of victims of the
moral darkness it brought to the 20th century*

*For
my parents
LAWSON and JOANNE
dear in memory*

Contents

Ideas have consequences.
Richard Weaver

How do we account for what has been called the
ideological frenzy of the twentieth century?
Robert Conquest

How the Journal of Mr. Darwin's Visitation Came to Light

THIS JOURNAL OF Charles Darwin, the great 19th century naturalist known to history as the author of the theory of the natural origin and evolution of life, is a record of his strange visit to earth in the Darwin Anniversary Year 2009. This astonishing testament came into my hands from the two young children of a friend returning from a transatlantic family trip to England that year. It is significant to this transaction that the children are descendants, in the fifth-generation, of the world-famous biologist--a relationship which bears on Mr. Darwin's serendipitous encounter with them, which his account will explain. It was Darwin himself--the children insistently say--who placed a bound, handwritten journal in their hands along the famous Sandwalk on the grounds of Down House, his much-visited home in the village of Downe, Kent.

As an interested observer of the 20th century world and its turn to a new millennium, I believed the profound reactions Mr. Darwin recorded in his journal--relating both to the social and ideological impact he observed his Idea to have had on the 20th century, and to the advent of the molecular biological revolution in the later decades of the century--merited this document's publication to the world.

In his journal, readers will find both personal and professional reflections on the vastly changed world revisited in 2009 by the author of *The Origin of Species* and *The Descent of Man*. Some may discover a Darwin they did not know, a sensitive, inquiring spirit whose thoughts and meditations are consonant with those expressed in his own *Life and Letters,* an autobiographical account which his son Francis edited and initially published in 1887, five years following Darwin's death. I have added an appendix of *personae* in order to identify Darwin's passing references to important contemporaries as well as to 20th-century figures whose activities and writings attracted his capacious powers of observation during his recent sojourn. Also appended is a list of certain writings he evidently consulted and chose to note in his testament's back pages, for which I have added publication data.

Ever an acute observer and assiduous pursuer of truth wherever it might lead--while alert always to contradiction and paradox in his famous Theory--Darwin has prefaced the chapters of his journal with citations taken from his *Origin* and his autobiography as well as citations he took from the writings of other observers of his own and our times.

Nickell John Romjue
Coventry, County of York, Virginia
June 2011

I

LONDON

I believe that I have acted rightly in steadily following and devoting my life to Science. I feel no remorse for having committed any great sin, but have often and often regretted that I have not done more direct good to my fellow creatures.

C.D.

WHEN I FOUND myself on earth again--the year, I soon discovered, was 2009--I was utterly perplexed. I remembered clearly the year of my passing, 1882. My bafflement was absolute. In my long life I had given little thought to an afterlife of any kind and certainly not to a terrestial reincarnation, which I had not witnessed in all my years of observing the natural and human world. What attention had I paid to the realm of spirit, or to superstition, reincarnations, seances? God? I believed my Theory probably had refuted with finality the notion of God, made him obsolete for posterity, though I respected his believers, in particular my sweet wife Emma, and indeed all our children were baptized in England's church.

And so was I confounded. Then I recalled, first dimly, then more clearly, the directive that had been given me. We are placing you down there again, *They* had said, for our own purposes. Not a little earth time has elapsed since your departure. Take another look. We value your gift for *dogged* observation. Do you perceive our touch of irony, They added, smiling--where did I think humor came from? But one thing, We forbid you. Observe only, remain anonymous, do not touch the lives of anyone living--We emphasize in particular--none of your descendants. We know human nature, don't We?

Even in my perplexity, I had to smile a little too. My "gift for *dogged* observation"--were They also reminding me of my great affection for my dogs, and maybe my boyish mortification too, when my father told me dogs were all I cared about along with shooting and rat-catching, and that I'd disgrace the family?

Then They told me to be sure to record my observations, which I didn't need to be instructed to do. Did They not remember my *Journal of Researches*--or as you know it, *Voyage of the Beagle*?

I found myself in a hotel room. There was a door that was all a mirror. Yes, it was me. My own face, my long, white beard, the dark suit of clothes I'd worn for my photographs, even the fur-lined slippers I wore over my shoes at Down House. Some sense of humor! I quickly kicked them off.

Reaching inside my coat, I found a wallet with currency--pound notes with the face of a beautiful queen, and other currency with faces that I recognized--Americans, their first great scientist Franklin, and George Washington, and General Grant.

I looked out my window. Where was I? There was the dome of St. Paul's, in the distance Westminster Abbey where, there had been some rumor, I was to be buried. There were shiny carriages on the street below--no horses! But I will not go further into that. It is *your* incomprehensible *technological* world--I am prepared for surprise and astonishment wherever I look. It is your *science* that I want to see.

Outside, I noticed immediately people staring at me--my long beard, my old-fashioned clothes. The first thing I did was suit myself into some of the strange, but comfortable, garments of your time. I left my black suit behind in the dressing booth. Then I found a barber shop and had my hair and beard severely trimmed. That was when I discovered a curious thing about my pound notes. Whatever notes I spent, I found new ones replaced straightaway in my wallet. This was no natural process. *They* were having quite a jest with me in my reincarnation in the year 2009. I had grasped the fact of the 200th marker of my birth, but only now did it occur to me--the 150th anniversary of the *Origin of Species*!

I soon discovered more suspensions of the laws of nature in my favor. By wishing it, I could transport myself instantly to any place on earth of which I knew or learned about. And I could will myself invisible.

But I had to be absolutely certain. I went on the instant to Westminster, and, yes, I was buried there--my tomb quite elaborately marked. And just a few steps from the bones of Sir Isaac Newton!

Outside, I bought a copy of the *Times*, I saw the front-page story, my picture, the sesquicentennial of *Origin*! And so it fully dawned on me--the "another look" was not about me. My privileged visitation was all about my *Idea*.

So here I am. Is my strange reincarnation or visitation or whatever it is--unique? Are there others? Metaphysics

is not my strength. I find myself, as you in the 21st century
are wont to say, in a "new normal." I seem to be absorb-
ing quite readily your odd lingo, though I will try to avoid
the excesses, which already appear to me to be many. I
am determined to do that which I know how to do, to observe, *doggedly,* with driving curiosity. I want to see how
my Idea advanced. And believing as I did that man in the
future would be a far more perfect creature than in my
time, I want to see just how my Idea may have changed
your world.

Or. . . do I find myself in some sort of posthumous
dreamworld? Am I a Rip Van Winkle awakening from the
effects of a flagon of elixirs I unknowingly quaffed in my
last month of life at Down? All around me, I seem to be
hearing thunder and rattle like the clatter of the dwarfs'
ninepins in Rip's mountain glen. No, it is only your motor carriages, wagons--lorries, I hear you call them, great
smoke-belching monsters I will need to be fit of foot to
survive in your hurly-burly world.

Yes, it *is* real. I have learned that I am *legend,* that what
I told the world has been consequential beyond my time
and beyond all imagining and in ways that place me in
profound shock. Yet, I am determined now to pursue, to
prosecute the inquiries flooding my mind, to the ends of
the earth. And I have a presentiment the thunder and clatter I hear may be of a tonal dimension beyond the raging
tempest of your street traffic, a thing of great moment.

In all of this, I marvel. I sought always the truth. I did
not anticipate what I have found in your world. And so in
this advanced year of the tumultous and riven times that

have succeeded my own, I will give you the results of the examination I have made of my legacy. My Idea, gripping the mind of the world, has changed the world in ways I find astounding. At the same time, my Idea, in its unfolding challenge, has encountered an intellectual revolution in your time.

And so I will tell you what I have learned about the origin and evolution of life and how it changed the world for the better or for the worse. For is science not forever the land of objective truth? Has science legitimacy if it blindly assumes the *a priori*, or asserts self-interest, or if it fails openness or self-criticism, if it stifles contradiction? Thus I leave this record for all who question, and especially for the questioning young to whom truth's future belongs. And I will leave this epistle to the generations of my grandchildren, two of whom I was privileged to meet after all and whom I love across legend and time.

II

THE *BEAGLE* AND GALAPAGOS

*As far as I can judge of myself, I worked to the utmost
during the voyage from the mere pleasure of investiga-
tion, and from my strong desire to add a few facts to the
great mass of facts in natural science.*

C.D.

*[T]he ground finches of the Galapagos Islands. . .more
than anything else persuaded Darwin of the fact of evolution.*

Julian Huxley

*[With Darwin's finches] [S]election oscillates with cli-
matic fluctuations, and does not exhibit long-term evolutionary change.*

Jonathan Wells

WHERE TO BEGIN my strange transplantation to your time, visitor from a distant era so heady with idea, pregnant with the future? I am reminded that my errand is earnest, my task a task of science--but perhaps more? The voyage of the H.M.S. *Beagle* was the most important event of my life. To it I owe all the sharpening of my powers of observation--my best virtue, in all due modesty. Indeed, when I returned from Captain FitzRoy's worldwide research odyssey, my father declared that the shape of my head was "quite altered"--and he was far from a phrenologist.

From the *Beagle* came the first three of my books, but it was, as you know, my observations in the isolated Galapagos Islands off the west coast of South America that would greatly buttress my seminal idea. Here, as in Australia's island, existed species of life seemingly related to mainland species but not found except in those isolated places. But what *had* I observed in the Galapagos and soon in Australia's examples of marsupial mammals found nowhere else in the world? I found life's fascinating capacity--when isolated from larger pools of life--to generate diversity, plenitude, new species.

Now, with my unlimited and apparently magical access to the work of my successors, I discovered on the Galapagos a curious turn of evolutionary events. Though I had not paid great attention to the species of finches I noted on our ship's stop there in 1835, textbooks of your time have made claim that my observations pointing to an evolution of finch-beak structure were the central inspiration for my Idea of natural selection. Did the finches of Galapagos demonstrate the principle of the evolution of one species into another, fitter species?

To my surprise, I learn that the evolutionary changes in the beaks of the Galapagos finches proved reversible. When the islands experienced seasons of heavier rainfall, propagating more and smaller seed varieties for the several finch species to feed upon, the evolutionary trend in those wet years was reversed to favor individuals with more pointed beaks. Natural selection here was an *oscillating* phenomenon. While species had evidently diverged, contingent on dry-wet weather cycles, they could apparently also merge, and indeed were doing just that.

Speciation does not occur when exclusive mating behavior--the true identifier of a separate species--proves flexible. I have noted too, in accounts of the spotted owl controversy of the American Northwest, that the wandering eye of this oddly newsworthy old-forest species has led it to mate outside the old-forest environment favoring its species, when it has been unable to locate a more agreeable spotted *in-species* mate.

I am struck by these interesting, if relatively trivial, findings. If in your time such contradictions have become observable in my *special* Theory limited to micro-change, what may be said about my great *general* Theory about evolution across the great divisions of life? I must ask, why do your textbooks ignore the empirical, contradictory evidence made manifest in the intensively measured observations of the merging and oscillating species of the Galapagos finches? I am finding my strange sojourn among you interesting and vexing. I am cheered by the assiduousness I encounter but perplexed by a sometime selectivity in the weighing of new evidence, a practice among you that baffles me. It quite violates our purposes.

I hold to my Theory. But in this first, fascinating foray into my renewed scientific life, I feel as if I have set out anew on the *Beagle*. What questions I have! I can hardly wait to learn what has evolved in every particular and general sense in this new age of the spread and application worldwide of the science of life.

In my sojourn I turned next, with great expectation, to the fossil testimony for my Idea. What would the record of the rocks say, the testament of earth's life in distant eras, which we were beginning to explore and document in my time? We had discovered many extinct forms of life and many primitive ancestors, we thought, of species living today. We believed the rock strata thus far found were revealing evidence of a steady and constant upward evolution from primitive forms to a seemingly numberless species of life.

But we had uncovered no transitional forms of life to solidify our encompassing classification system. Certainly, 150 years' passage would yield a plenitude of the theretofore missing links in the great divisions of life.

III

THE FOSSILS

[I]f the theory be true, it is indisputable that before the lowest Cambrian stratum was deposited long periods elapsed, as long as, or probably far longer than, the whole interval from the Cambrian age to the present day; and that during these vast, yet quite unknown periods of time, the world swarmed with living creatures.

[The lack of transitional forms is] the most obvious and serious objection which can be urged against the theory.

C.D.

It is as though they [the phyla formed at the beginning of the Cambrian Explosion] were just planted there, without any evolutionary history.

Richard Dawkins

I AM MOST expectantly excited as I take up the texts of my worthy paleontologist successors. For in these 150 years, theirs has been, I learned, one of the "growth industries" of science. I yield here again to the sometimes charming evolutionary turns of our remarkable English language. And I have now learned to use your "worldwide web," so fascinated was I by this magical research tool when I first saw it in use in one of your libraries. When I hovered invisibly but too close over the shoulder of a fellow at this computer instrument, my shortened bristly beard managed to brush his neck, sending the poor man from the place screaming. Cancelling out the pornographic images (!!) he was watching, I went right to work.

It was on the amazing worldwide web that I found a listing of all the major fossil sites, now excavated in the many hundreds and on every continent including even Antarctica and on many of the earth's island groups.

As I have noted, naturalists and geologists had in my time uncovered a fossil panoply of long extinct life forms, along with others appearing clearly as ancestral to modern species. Those remains had aided the piecing together of a comprehensive classification system by which we could reckon and name the ages of the earth and the divisions of life back to the early rock strata we termed the Cambrian. In that record, we theorized and sought, in the similarities of skeletal body structures, a grand evolution of life from an earliest unicellular form upward to the first, primitive species, branching then to new species within common genera and to their further branching in an increase of genera, forming families, orders, classes to be gathered into major phyla of life within the plant and animal kingdoms. That was the fixed idea which I--and Wallace too, about the same time--successfully buttressed. As I pointed out, we awaited the fossil finds that would provide the fuller record of transitional forms that had to have existed as links in the evolution of life's major divisions across time. I will say that my naturalist friend Agassiz noted, quite early, problems for my Theory with what we knew then about the Cambrian.

Thus I read voraciously in your sources and texts. With the special powers granted me, I visited many fossil sites, for I knew the record of the rocks was hardly to be disputed.

It is with utter astonishment that I observe that that record, explored intensively throughout the globe in the century and a quarter since I departed, fails to produce the intermediate forms! There are no transitional fossilized forms linking the major divisions over the past 500 million years! Not one unquestioned missing link in the myriad of intermediate forms, which my Theory demanded, has been found. Not in the famous Burgess Shale of British Columbia, or in the Ediacaran Hills of South Australia, or elsewhere--no fossils documenting the skeletal and organ changes necessary to demonstrate evolution across the great schematic of life.

Rather than a graduated timeline of all earth's species from the earliest life forms to the latest, which my Theory established, you made in the early part of your century a stunning discovery. That was the appearance--suddenly in geological time, with no ancestors, of the body plans of living animal forms extant in the world today, along with the multitude of those long extinct. The "Cambrian Explosion" of life, which the multiple excavated sites all revealed, showed animal phyla as distinct from each other as they are today!

It appeals to one's sense of irony, but hardly to professional propriety, that your paleontologist Gould so forthrightly quipped that the Cambrian Explosion was "the trade secret of paleontology."

At major excavation sites, from the Burgess Shale discovered in 1909 to the comprehensive Chengjiang finds in Yunnan Province in China in the 1980s, there were no pre-Cambrian ancestor forms. In those earlier strata, only simple unicellular and primitive multi-cellular forms appear. Radiometric dating of formations just above and below Cambrian strata at another Cambrian site, in Siberia, set the Cambrian Explosion of life at 530 million years ago.

What can this mean? It appears to mean that the great phyla of the animal kingdom known to us did not evolve "bottom-up" from earlier, more primitive forms. The Cambrian Explosion documented in the strata reveals the opposite. The phyla came first--life on earth diversified from the Cambrian phyla "top-down"! Moreover, most species appear fully formed and, it has been established, do not change from the time of their first appearance in the fossil record until they disappear from it.

I visited the Burgess and Chengjiang sites, and others, just to assure myself that they really existed. And I examined closely your documentation, all the while recalling what I had written in the opus by which I had introduced my signal Idea to the world: "If numerous species, belonging to the same genera or families, have really started into life all at once, the fact would be fatal to the theory of descent with slow modification through natural selection."

Here indeed is a "genesis age," Biblical Genesis or naught, whose record in the strata stands in utter contradiction to my Theory. I am stupefied, but I am cheered, for science must of needs be elated by great factual discoveries. I face the evidence here of a fundamental denial by the fossil record of the grand upward-branching Tree of Life. The world is deeper than even Nietzsche imagined--yes, I could not have failed in my sojourn to have looked into Nietzsche, who indicated his debt to my Idea.

But I could hardly believe "my lying eyes," as one of your American humorists has put it, and so I examined closely the theories and examples related to the missing links--the transitional intermediate forms upon which my "bottom-up" Theory depended. I hoped to encounter if not evidence, then some plausible explanation.

In this inquiry, I was taken by an assertion that the amazingly complex avian feather structure which I studied had evolved from a reptilian "frayed" scale. What could have been the intermediates involved on the way to the perfection of the feather, with its unique system of coadapted components? I paraphrase briefly from the plentiful literature your biologists have given you. Such presumedly evolving appendages of reptile-to-bird intermediates on their way from one well-operating function (ground mobility) to a much different well-operating function (flight) would surely have resulted in clumsy and non-functional appendages and, therefore, fatalities in nature's competition. Does not such an intermediate appendage (and there would have to have been many successively improved such appendages) necessarily signify dysfunction, and with dysfunction, not evolution, but the end of the line?

I note a latter-day way around the problem, the "punctuated equilibrium" notion advanced by Gould. It says nature made "jumps". Here is the problem: How can the incipient evolving structure, say, of one part of a creature, a part previously so obviously and beautifully adapted to and integrally meshed with all the other parts of the same creature, make its sudden appearance--without retarding fatally the so marvelously integrated whole organism? I find no shred of empirical evidence existing to support saltational jumps, an equivalent to the "multiple universes" that some of your astronomers fancifully rationalize based on naught empirical evidence.

What remains of my "gradualism"? The incontestable record of the Cambrian Explosion and the failure of fossil evidence for intermediates that might have buttressed my Theory leaves me with gaps of logic that cannot be closed.

The gaps are overwhelming. I am left with a stunning conclusion. The major structures of the living world are discontinuous. Just as in your pioneering world of particle physics, in which one cannot change one sort of atom into another, so there is, in the living world, no grand continuum. Nature is ruled by discontinuities.

But I am further troubled by something here. I find a marked strangeness in Gould's witty "trade secret" admission, which I noted earlier. What does biology--indeed all science--have to do with secrets, concealments? In the amazing printed and electronic media and three-dimensional fauna reconstructions of your time in the British and American-Smithsonian museums of natural history and elsewhere, I see, in 2009, the Tree of Life faithfully reproduced everywhere--as if the Cambrian Explosion of life had never occurred! And I marvel at the sheer asserted totality that your evolutionary data portrayals imply as present in the fossil record.

Particularly, I am drawn to the dramatic portrayals of the "march to man," the subject I elucidated to great ensuing controversy in my *Descent*. I refer to the image sequence one sees everywhere of the march from simian forms through many named stages of hominid evolution to arrival at the gates of civilization--modern *Homo sapiens*. One of the portrayals reminded me of the wild Fuegians I observed in our Cape Horn expeditions in 1833, who at that late date appeared not to have achieved that milestone. What astonishing finds there must have been since my passing to have yielded the evolutionary odyssey of our species so dramatically portrayed in your museums.

It was with surprise and disappointment that I examined, sometimes surreptitiously, the assembled bone specimens identifying the ancestors of man. I examined the famous Leakey bone fragments and associated "rival" fragments, among others. I do not say willingly that I was astonished by the paucity and incompleteness of many of the skull fragments and skeletal pieces I found in the research drawers by means of my special access. Perhaps paucity is another sometime trade secret.

I found that the scant collection of putatively pre-human skull fragments demonstrates no evidential sequence of evolutionary development whatsoever. Rather, they are placed into pre-existing narratives of the march to man. I ask: are your paleoanthropologists scientists, or are they storytellers who seem constantly in celebration of new "first" humans--in turn ensuring disputes?

As recently as two years ago, paleontologists in Tanzania discovered, in close physical proximity, skull fragments of *Homo erectus* and *Homo habilis,* the former's previously asserted ancestor. Must someone not now inform the artists of the heroic march to man cartoons to redraw the family tree, since the two putatively successive species may actually have lived side by side? The "sticking points" (another example of a nicely evolved phrase) here are an evidently shaky, not to say specious sequence, and short-lived "firsts". An amazing example announced to great fanfare, I read with interest, was "Lucy", whose remains were discovered in Ethiopia in 1974 and once styled the "grandmother of humanity." I observed her retired cache of bones, carefully secured from public gaze in a safe in Addis Ababa, to which I had special access.

One must be reminded that a set of hominid scraps are often the remains of a single individual. How does one convincingly extrapolate such data to a new species claim? In the well-reported finds of some paleontology "celebrities" of your era, it appears to me that the passage from suggestive data to evidential certitude has been remarkable. I am quite taken by the competitive ring and brief life of these assured claims, and their attendant reputational displacements.

I believe that the beckoning chalice of the "first man," which paleoanthropologists so ambitiously seek, clouds a greater paleontological truth. It is not the march to man that they have secured. Rather, they are discovering one specimen after another of nature's Mendelian diversity. They are finding the ever-branching diversity exhibited *within two hominid forms,* similar in body plan but distinct in the most significant distinction in the living world: that which separates humanity from all other life.

In my time I was greatly struck by the amazing diversity in the physiognomy and underlying skull structure even of *19th century Homo sapiens* throughout the globe, indeed even in Europe. Now, I note the recent DNA evidence (I will speak more on that subject later) that one of man's variously theorized predecessor or companion species, Neanderthal, indeed mated with Homo sapiens. A minor percentage of Europeans today carry some Neanderthal genes, even as the appearance of Neanderthal-like visages on the streets of European cities may be observed. But does not interbreeding negate separate-species classification?

I see here a sometime casualness I had not expected to find. What is evidence, uncritically weighed? in my lifetime I believed my own findings indicated an important theory; but I did not fit findings *to* theory. Science is never not complex, but it can never be tendentious. One may not present to the museum public, and to schoolchildren, texts and reconstruction images as if they possessed the authenticity of photographic reality.

I speak only briefly of paleontology scandals large and small that have marred the record since I last breathed 19th century air--the fraudulent reconstruction of specimens from parts known to be unrelated. The most prominent, I discovered with dismay, is the so-called "Piltdown Man," an inventive assembly of the jaw of a modern orangatan chemically treated to appear as a fossil,with skull fragments of a modern human. Its zealous inventors succeeded in touting it to the believing public for over 40 years as the long-sought missing link between simian and man. An evolutionary scientist in the British Museum assembled the fraudulent skull! One may only weep.

IV

THE TREE

All the organic beings which have ever lived on this earth may be descended from some one primordial form.

C.D.

LET ME SAY that during my lifetime I observed contradictions in my Theory. I fully expected them to find future resolution. But who can deny that the record of the rocks, which I have just noted, fundamentally contradicts the whole schematic that grew and thrived on my Idea? I shall make my point simple. The be-all and end-all Tree of Life encompassing the origin and descent of every present and extinct species based on structural similarities--the bat's wing to the human hand, for example--is a metaphor which the evidence no longer supports. In my surreptitious and sometimes open visits not only to your university lecture rooms and laboratories but to such interesting places as the biogenetic croplands and the blue-ribbon purebred competitions of the state fairs of the American Midwest, I find ever new modern locutions to copy as I seek to develop this testament of my unusual sojourn. Allow me to apply one of them, an expression I overheard at an American state fair--Missouri, I believe. I must aver that the Tree of Life is as conceptually misleading indeed as--forgive me--"a tit on a boar hog"!

Similar body parts like the bat-wing/human-hand example, we call homologous structures. Where homology was detectable, my Theory inferred a common ancestor of the ever-branching forms of life descending through slow and slight modifications by natural selection. This was blind nature's way of selecting the most fit, the most adaptable, to survive.

Sometimes I liked to taunt my religion-inspired contemporaries about the pentadactyl pattern I observed in the limbs of the major terrestial vertebrates. Why would a Creator feel constrained to hold to such a rigid template, if He could "do anything"? The inference here is that homology proved common descent. Now, I find that a branch of my succession, your embryologists, have utterly upended my certitude. They have found that the embryology of the three classes of vertebrates--amphibians, reptiles, mammals--denies the homology principle. For example, organs such as vertebrate kidneys in disparate life forms cannot be traced back to homologous cells. Seemingly similar or homologous structures have distinctly non-homologous beginnings in their respective embryos.

Here is a finding that further shook my faith in the Tree. Most genes--which of course, as my successors have established, determine the characteristics of the next generation--affect in higher organisms *more than one organ system*. Genes are non-homologous. But is not the concept of homology absolutely fundamental to my Idea, indeed to evolutionary theory today? The resemblances among species, which I took to demonstrate homology--nature's modification of similar structures to different purposes--lies at my Theory's very heart. My evidence was circumstantial.

Indeed I am now struck by the patently circular reasoning process my Idea actually demands. The theory of descent from a common ancestor requires a subsequent evolution of similar or homologous structures, and those structures, when they emerge, prove common descent. Homology is inferred from common ancestry, and is then used as evidence for common ancestry, as one of your biologists has pointed out. Theory requires the outcome, and the outcome confirms the theory. In my sojourn with you, I sometimes rested my brain by scanning your incredible television commercials. I will mention an apropos line: "What was I thinking"?

There is no credible Tree of Life. The Cambrian Explosion negates it, and the discontinuities of presumed homologous structures refute it The crashing of the Great Tree in the forest of contentious, truth-seeking science has hurt my ears.

This much remains. Natural selection occurs on the micro scale, that is, within species and, in instances, beyond the species barrier. The environmental advantage for dominance or survival gained by individuals of a species favored by breeding's diverse gene selection is documented in human historical time. There are observed instances of evolutionary change resulting in emergence of new species, as in the European gull through its many-generational migration across Eurasia. And yet some new species, as defined by their preferential breeding behavior, are observed to interbreed with "ancestor" species.

In my on-the-scene investigations at the Burgess Shale and Chengjiang, as well as in your imaginative storytelling natural-history presentations, I found much to deepen skepticism as to my initial premises and assumptions of 1859. And yet in my odyssey in your remarkable age of baffling human behavior and intellectual idolatries, more than disappointment lay ahead in my amazing adventure.

V

NATUR IST ALLES, ALLES IST NATUR

At some future period, not very distant as measured in centuries, the civilized races of man will almost certainly exterminate and replace throughout the world the savage races.

C.D.

Man is, in substance and in structure, one with the brutes.

Thomas H. Huxley

The Origin of Species introduced a mode of thinking that in the end was bound to transform the logic of knowledge and hence the treatment of morals, politics, and religion.

John Dewey

GALAPAGOS, THE *BEAGLE* and my youth; the fossil record; homology's claim and the Tree of Life--these were the first errands of my time-transcending visitation. All induced in me profound astonishment. My next discovery, I did not seek out. I now note the great, unexpected impact of my Idea *beyond* science.

It did not escape me that the philosophical and religious implications of my *Origin* and *Descent* would have wider historical effects. The reactions of my dear wife Emma to my to-be-famous Theory are well known. The very idea, advanced earlier in my century by Feuerbach, Comte, and others, of a reality of existence that owed wholly to material cause--that idea acquired in my evolutionary Theory the seal of science. My Idea, posing an all-encompassing naturalism to explain life's origin and evolution, needed no God. it displaced our old civilization's Story of Creation and reduced the Scriptures and the God that spoke from them to products of the human imagination. Such was the impact on Christian belief of my revolutionary Idea. This, I say in due modesty. That I would become legend in your time, as I have discovered, I attribute to my convincing demonstration *in nature* of the power of a fundamental idea.

But I did not anticipate the scale of the power that my Idea would achieve *beyond* the realm of science. Before I died, I had seen clearly how the concept of the evolutionary Tree of Life was igniting the imagination of the educated middle and upper classes in England, Europe, the United States, indeed all the Western World and beyond. I attracted the staunchist and most combative of disciples--Huxley in my own land and Haeckel in Germany. My Idea and its derivatives--the material origin (though still undiscovered) of the first, primitive life form, the survival of the fittest in nature's competition through natural selection, which I adapted from Malthus's population theory--these concepts together put in place the basis of a new paradigm of reality which the world, recalling Aristotle, termed materialism or philosophical naturalism.

Let me say that I was hardly the sole creator of the paradigm either in its origin or its steady advancement. The announcement of other major idea systems preceded, paralleled, and followed mine: Comte's disarraying positivism; Hegel's seal on the inevitability of historical processes; the classes and masses gospel of Marx; the, let me call it, animalistic explanation of human behavior that characterized the thought system of Freud; and, yes, the elevation of man to the morally-free *overman* by Nietzsche. All these great displacing ideologies joined with the social implications of my own Idea to create and to implant in the modern mind a belief that all reality, all objects, even all thoughts generated by the human brain were products of purely material processes. As my enthusiastic German disciple Haeckel put it: *Natur ist Alles, Alles ist Natur.* Nature is all, everything is nature.

The materialist paradigm whose scientific basis I established gave, in turn, philosophical legitimacy to those ideologies, which in your 20th century would evolve into passionate belief systems influencing the conduct and life of powerful states and the lives of hundreds of millions of human beings. Of those thought/belief systems, the most durable, if embattled in its 150th anniversary year, is "Darwinism"--my general Theory of Evolution.

I did not foresee that my Theory would evolve as an ideology, a belief system. "Evolution" itself, I have learned, evolved in ways beyond all expectation after I left the world, bursting the bonds of strict science to become in Herbert Spencer's "Social Darwinism" a school of philosophy and social action and, like Marxism and Freudianism, for many a veritable religion.

A religion! Who in my day would have guessed that I--of whom a zealous biologist of your time has said that I made it "philosophically respectable to be an atheist"-- who would have guessed that I would one day be worshipped?!! "Darwin Day" indeed! I am a scientist, not an idol! Though I will note that my contemporaries Karl, Sigmund, and Friedrich assumed and indeed magnified their idol roles quite readily--Nietzsche not so happily, passing his last years, I have learned, "off his chump," as Englishmen put it so charmingly. I have read extensively of the legacies of Marx and Freud. Were they perhaps off their chump to begin with? I have learned things about their legacies, and about mine, that I did not wish to know. My Idea indeed put something new into the world that I did not foresee.

Did any of us anticipate the unexpected and lethal payment that would fall due for the world after we had stripped man of his historical belief, millennia old, in a transcendent universal morality?

I find myself in a world I helped to make. I say this with no false modesty. I do not like all that I see. What are we as scientists if we abjure the objective weighing of new factual data? Science is honesty, or it is nothing. It compels us to reassess even foundational ideas, ideas that generated a panoply of human disaster from the early 20th century almost to its end. Ideas that indeed rule, still in part, the modern world.

About that sad and tragic subject, I shall now put down my shocked observations, before turning to the scientific revolution that your violent and brilliant century has given the world.

VI

BEAST TO BEAST

God is dead; we have killed him with our science.

Friedrich Nietzsche

[Ethics is] an illusion fobbed off on us by our genes.

Michael Ruse

The scientific concept of dictatorship remains nothing else but this: Power without limit, resting directly upon force, restrained by no laws, absolutely unrestricted by rules.

Vladimir [Ilyich] Lenin

LUPUS EST HOMO homini. That man is a wolf to man is our inheritance from brute Nature. Yet in my time we believed man would break the bonds as superstition was overcome and ignorance disappeared. For us an age of reason and progress had dawned.

Certainly there were reminders that the full enlightenment of humanity still lay ahead. Chattel slavery lived on in parts of the world even after the American Civil War, and the terrible carnage of that war recalled to us Europe's bloodiest rivalries of the past. And yet, the recent German Wars of Unification had been relatively bloodless. And the march of science and industry, the beneficent reach of our civilization throughout the globe--these augeries of enlightened times were everywhere observable. Historians were concluding that ours was indeed "The Century of Progress."

How does one account for the age that followed mine, a century of violence of unprecedented dimension? When I learned of the savage World Wars and the horrific genocides and democides--the killing by ideological regimes of scores upon scores of millions of men, women, and children that befell the world in the 20th century--I read

those accounts of human destruction on a scale beyond
any century in modern history, in a state of disbelief and
utter shock. I could not grasp the scale of savagery--a *civilized* savagery--that had overtaken the world. Your century, your times were the "sunny posterity" forecast by
the Enlightenment philosophers!

I could not grasp this monumental reversal in the descent of humankind. That we were evolved from beasts,
I firmly believed. Indeed in my time there were still "un-
explored" markings on the maps--there were savage
peoples still undiscovered. I think of my Fuegians, more
vicious toward each other than the species of the apes.
But by the onset of the 20th century, the impediments to
ignorance and superstition in most places were largely
fallen away.

I weep as I read of the gas chambers, the great death
camps and gulags, the very industrialization of the killing
of races and classes and hapless masses--and not by the
agency of your incomparably destructive World Wars, but
in coldly planned and executed mass killings of unwanted
populations separate from the activity of war. How does
one explain history's descent into the greatest killing time
the world has ever seen?

Hitler's Auschwitz and its sister extermination camps
in the 1940s; Lenin's and Stalin's forced famines and vast
killing network, its Gulag Archipelago, across bloody
decades from the 1920s to the 1960s; Mao's Great Leap
Forward in the late 1950s with its 20 million dead; the bestial jungle democides in the 1970s of Pol Pot, Cambodian
revolutionary schooled in Paris, capital of the quintessen-

tial Western nation. And many, many others, too numerous to note here. How did evolution's most advanced,
highest form of life--*Homo sapiens:* beautiful children,
women, men--come to be so devalued that they were
rounded up to be exterminated like rats?

I ask myself and I ask you: how in the year 2009 do you
live with this legacy, so fresh in the memory of your older
generations? Does the horror of your century--for you are
but nine years beyond it--does the horror not shout out at
you? I have visited your museums and monuments dedi-
cated to National Socialism's Holocaust of the European
Jews, and one is stricken to entertain the horror. But where
are the museums and monument reminders of the, by mul-
tiples greater, democides by revolutionary socialism, the
Communist killer-states, the greatest of which was over-
thrown only twenty years ago? Where is your memory of
cause and consequence? Does it require a time traveller to
make you think?

Did Marx foresee where his idea would lead in its
application by Lenin and Stalin, Mao, Ho Chi Minh, Pol
Pot, and their imitators--to the cold, statist execution of
110 million and more powerless human beings worldwide? Marx, possessed of a closed mind frozen in dialec-
tic, grandfather of unspeakable brutalities. Here is what
he said of my *Origin:* "Darwin's book is very important
and serves me as a basis for the class struggle in history." Marx asked to dedicate his famously influential *Das
Kapital* to me! I said, No. How glad I am! I have learned
that Marx's text, scoring capitalism as history's great de-
nier of equality, sedulously avoided discussion of the ori-

gins of totalitarian socialism in the great ant states of the Ancient World. Marxism was not just anti-private property, it attacked the family, and religion--you should read *The Communist Manifesto.*

And Freud in his long reign, I have learned, believing his system a replacement for Moses and Christ, effectively derationalized humanity. He reduced people to hapless creatures of instincts that were not to be denied. "Man is not different from or better than the animals." Did the *Doktor* grasp the consequences of legitimizing, placing foremost, the animal in man? Currency notes of enlightened Austria today bear the face of Freud, who also acknowledged his intellectual debt to me, so it appears.

The dreamer Nietzsche has blessed me too for my founding Idea of the birth of humanity from the womb of a materialist world. Announcing in his siren song the funeral of God and the removal of all traditional moral restraint, he announced the devolution of evolution's most advanced life form--to a species of higher-order beast. I read of Nietzsche's fools today, morally free *overmen* who climb mountain peaks and write heroically in their diaries as they bravely die, caught in the ice storms.

These tributes amaze and repel me. I did not seek them. My passion was earth's life--its fascinating mystery. What is the meaning of the tributes? What is the meaning of the so-well-documented impact of my Idea *beyond* biology? Am I a creator too of riven modern man? "God is dead," Nietzsche wrote. "We have killed him with our science." *Whose science?* I ask.

My Idea shook the scientific world. Its implication

dislodged religious belief and installed a radically new lens through which the world would view all reality from the very beginning of life on earth to the most fundamental philosophical and religious questions. It allowed for no Creation and no God. It allowed for a morality not universal for all men, but contingent in time, place, cultural circumstance. It reconstructed human values, even good and evil, as human inventions. All is relative, *Alles ist Natur.*

Here is what the young seminary student Iosif Dzhugashvili, Stalin-to-be, is said to have exclaimed when he discovered my Idea--so the biography he endorsed tells us: "They've tricked us all along. There is no God." Lenin, creator of the Soviet totalitarian state, kept a little statue on his desk--an ape sitting on a pile of books including mine, gazing at a human skull. And Mao Zedong, butcher of the tens of millions of his own countrymen, who regarded the German *"Darwinismus"* writings as the foundation of Chinese "scientific socialism." This disciple mandated my works as reading material for the indoctrination phase of his lethal Great Leap Forward.

The powerful impact of my writings on the German mind through Haeckel and others is well known. Their impact was fundamental to the rise of eugenics in Germany, Great Britain, as well as in the United States, and elsewhere. Indeed my own cousin Galton--drawing on my Idea--was the founding spirit of modern eugenics!

It is beyond dispute that my Idea, filtered through the eugenics and racial strains of social Darwinism, powerfully affected Hitler's genocidal policies and racial superiority-based war-making. Hitler thoroughly absorbed my struggle-for-existence notions. One need only consult his famous early memoir. For him, traditional transcendent, universal morality had no objective existence. Evolutionary ethics to eugenics to racial extermination. For the theoreticians of National Socialism, the thought sequence is undeniable. Scholars of Nazism almost universally acknowledge my baleful influence on Hitler. My Theory altered the way people thought about morality. It was a major contributor to the moral relativism whose acolytes flourished as beasts of the modern world.

Would those great malefactors have formulated their disastrous dreams without me--I who made blind nature the Creator? Is it I who *unGodded* modern man, dissolved the objective moral world, set in motion the great wheel of the violent 20th century? Darwin, Marx, Nietzsche, Freud--were we indeed the Four Horsemen of the century of apocalypse for so many millions?

An American historian, Sontag, has written of your "broken world," the period after the First World War, when the new thought systems I have noted jelled into adamant, self-sealed totalist ideologies, evolving as lethality-dispensing state regimes that claimed and commanded total political and moral authority. I read of the unGodded power-states that carried out the monumental crimes, regimes which assumed to themselves the mantle of higher moral authority, permitting all things.

A conviction grips me that the world's greatest loss in your time was the relativizing of morality, the putative killing of God. Nietzsche showed prescience when he articulated in 1887 his prophecy for the age ahead: the "ruin" of Christian morality, "that great spectacle in one hundred acts, which remain reserved for the next two centuries." What would Nietzsche say if he could return as I have been privileged to do, if he could return at the midpoint of his great doom prophecy?

I ask again: Am I not party to that great killing, perhaps more than the others? Was it not I who gave scientific endorsement to the death of God, that is, that his existence was but inventive myth? It was with great pain that I discussed that implication of my Idea with my beloved wife. She was in deepest distress. And yet, I could not compromise what my Theory rationalized--supported, I believed, by closest observation.

And so I do not shirk recognition of my legacy. Science asks all questions. I have read intensively in my year with you. I have haunted your libraries and laboratories. Some of you have reported fleeting glimpses of me in my previous incarnation. It seems I sometimes "revert" when I grow excited, when what I discover to have happened since 1882 literally takes my breath away.

What is my legacy? I am a founder, I am a destroyer. My revelation dechristianized, secularized the mind of the 20th century and beyond, nullifying mankind's need for a Creator God. My Idea was electrifying like nothing that had gone before. Through the 1880s and 1890s, I learn from your historians, thousands upon thousands of the educated classes of Europe and North America and beyond ceased to believe in the God of History, in the miraculous atoning resurrection of Christ the God-man, and in any transcendent reality. Man and not an invented God came to stand at the summit of reality as life's highest form, evolved to his station in accordance with an iron law of nature that I had made believable to mankind. My revolution gave birth to scientism--the encompassing by science of all reality.

I did not see the unintended consequence--the decivilizing of man, his devaluation to hapless product of a blind, accidental and random material process utterly without meaning in a meaningless universe.

What more can I say--your World Wars, your long Cold War to defeat a totalitarian socialism, and in 2009 a new, second long war which you must wage, if you are to survive against a fanatical jihadist Islam that arms itself to obliterate you with your own technology. And not only its foil, the "Crusader" West, but *you*--the unGodded, secular, enlightened West! How will you steel yourself against that assault if you believe that all things, most of all the values of your hard-crafted civilization, are accidental and relative, with no special claim to exist over any other?

I had not reckoned with the social and political force that my Idea would generate in the world. I have studied your demythologizers, of which so many emerged. How rapidly did your new God-substitutes appear, claimants to absolute moral authority over you, authority previously possessed by the now dead God, as Nietzsche confidently put it. I studied these developments incredulously.

Man to Overman, to demigod, to embodiment of highest moral authority in an accidental, Godless universe, apogee of evolution, killer of his devalued "nonhuman" fellowmen in extermination camps and chambers by the scores of millions--men, women, beautiful children and, yes, babies in the womb. Beast to beast in the most advanced of all centuries and eras. History weeps.

VII

THE CELL'S SECRET

[The cell is a] simple little lump of albuminous combination of carbon. . . .

Ernst Haeckel

[The tiniest bacterial cell] is in effect a veritable micro-miniaturized factory containing thousands of exquisitely designed pieces of intricate molecular machinery, made up altogether of one hundred thousand million atoms, far more complicated than any machine built by man and absolutely without parallel in the non-living world.

Michael Denton

We have found the secret of life.

Francis Crick

BUT HOW STRANGE the paradox that your century and time of bestial democides also developed as an age of stunning scientific discoveries and applications. Particle physics and the splitting of the atom, relativity, the Big Bang beginnings of our universe of billions of galaxies, space travel, moon and Mars landings, electric and petroleum-based motive power, heavier-than-air flight, jet aircraft, radio, radar, television, and cybernetics, computers and their vast application, all linked in a worldwide earth-satellite web of communications and knowledge, and your conquest of the many lethal diseases of mankind, your fantastic healing medicines, antibiotics, the molecular biological revolution.

I do not hope to understand the development or impact of those almost numberless marvels, which have utterly transformed human life since my time. The mind cannot encompass the great plenitude of scientific and technological genius that marked the 20th century. It is for only one of all those creations of the age that I have been privileged to see, for which I may claim competence to inquire into. I speak of the unlocking of the secret of the cell, the fundamental structure of life. For revealed within the

cell as we now know is the key to the origin of species and
the crux of the question of evolution.

When I encountered the "DNA revolution," it took my
breath away! I had to lie down--so fast was my heart beat-
ing--for twenty minutes. I felt that all the drawers of my
mind had opened at the same time. Had I not previously
trimmed my "signature" beard as I have told you, I would
have pulled it like a madman. I liken this moment--now
with some irony--to the dawning on my mind of my own
consequential Idea when I was young.

For what I perceived immediately was that the cell of
life, a virtually impenetrable blob of living matter seen
through the crude microscopes of my time, that this astonishing complex of intricate, interworking miniature
mechanisms replete with its own inbuilt information storage and processing system and creative, self-replicating
powers, was not only the central key to all the evolutionary change that my Theory had proposed. It was also a
structure whose astonishing intricacy and interdependent
complexity presented fundamental difficulties to the very
causation crux of my Idea: that is to say, the impact of a
random mutation on the heretofore unimagined, complex,
integrated whole--the truly vast machine-like complex of
the cell. And the organs and other components of almost
all living forms were constituted of many kinds of cells!

"If it could be demonstrated," I had said, "that any
complex organ existed which could not possibly have
been formed by numerous, successive, slight modifications, my theory would absolutely break down." My Idea,
drawing somewhat on Lamarck's notion of inheritable or

acquired characteristics, was "pangenesis." I held that hereditary particles in our bodies were affected by things we did during our lifetime. The modified particles migrated through the blood to the reproductive cells, to be inherited by the next generation.

Of course, I had never dreamed of the idea of a molecular basis of life. Nor had my early successors, who in the first part of your century altered my theory of descent somewhat. Rediscovering the assiduous genetic research of the Moravian monk Mendel, published in 1866, of which I had known nothing, they infused into my Theory the idea that natural selection acted on the random variations or mutations specifically in the genetic material of organisms.

Mendel's research with many generations of garden peas proved that it was not acquired parent characteristics, but laws of genetic selection that determined the traits of subsequent generations. The inheritance of a trait was determined, he said, by "factors", which subsequently came to be called genes. Mendel's and later research viewed evolutionary change to occur specifically *in the genetic text* as the key to my natural selection principle over vast periods leading to whole new phyla of life. Thus did Darwinism as evolutionary theory, itself evolve into "neo-Darwinism." And yet, with the DNA molecular revolution to come, something of greater moment lay on the horizon. I describe it now to clear my disbelieving mind. Here, I paraphrase my esteemed successors.

Every living cell, of whatever type, has the same basic biochemical structure, from bacteria to the disparate cells

of our own organism. The very roles of the cell's components are identical. At the heart of each cell is a set of direc-
tions coded in an internal structure called a double helix,
discovered by Watson and Crick in 1953. It is formed of
a compound, deoxyribonucleic acid, or DNA. The DNA
molecule consists of four nucleotides arrayed across the
double helix in many combinations specifying the functions that their coded information activates in the cell.

The DNA molecule, only about one infinitesimal nano-
meter thick, would be if stretched out, one meter long! The
information it contains is encyclopedic--a genetic code
distinct not only for the species, but for each individual of
the species!

The specific information the DNA contains, which is
then translated and transmitted by ribonucleic acid, or
RNA, messenger molecules, is actually automated information telling the cell what to do. DNA is the cell's blueprint. RNA carries the DNA's information to those parts
of the cell that manufacture the cell's functional machines-
-the proteins--telling them how to construct themselves
for the many functionally specified complex tasks that the
proteins carry out. I am not an emotional man, but these
revelations, for me, make Galapagos appear like a Sunday
stroll!

The proteins are the workhorses of the cell, the real
stuff of life. Each of them is a molecular micro-machine
that one would have to magnify a million times to see.
Each consists of a chain-like molecule, or polymer--a sequence of twenty or so compounds--amino acids. Every
different protein has a unique acid sequence and is a

three-dimensional folded chain subject to different kinds of electro-chemical forces that facilitate the atomic interactions between the amino acids that enable the functioning of the particular type of protein. Substitution of one type of amino acid in the chain for another destabilizes the entire molecule. Proteins are folded within the cell into immensely complex spatial arrangements.

But the interoperability of protein functions within the cell adds a further dimension of complexity. The molecules of cellular proteins operate not singly, but in teams. The functioning of any particular type of cell requires the successful binding, or interaction, of constituent proteins. Your researchers today say that random evolution of such protein-to-protein binding--that is to say, a coinciding mutational change in the complex structures of two proteins simultaneously--is mathematically beyond the reach of chance.

I learn that there are proteins which, one must say, possess a programmatic genius. These are homeotic or "hox" proteins--master regulators or switches that in sequence turn on animal development programs from embryo to adult. I think now of the charming mystery in my own children's little smiles when, having lost their baby teeth, their new ones began to appear. Hox proteins do their work in fruit flies, and they do their work in humans--in our body plans, beginning during our nine months' gestation programs. They build our marvelous organs and limbs, all our parts, down to the hair follicles of facial skin that have provided so luxuriantly for me in my high maturity.

What are the functions the cell of life fulfills? Here
is how your biologists describe the process. The cell is
a complex of molecular machines. They haul "cargo"
along infinitesimal "highways." They operate biochemical "switches" that regulate the entry and exit of materials
from the cell. They capture energy, allowing electric current to flow. They build other machines that, for example,
ingest food. I cite you molecular geneticist Denton.

How did I theorize the way evolutionary change
comes to a species? The kernal of my Idea was that when
a favorable random mutation occurred in an individual of
a species, it gave that individual and its progeny a greater
survival advantage against competitors in the struggle for
existence. And so did the whole species evolve over time
through accumulation of such random occurrences. I did
not know the mechanism by which I believed that to occur. But now we know the mechanics and constituents of
the process.

In a word, it is in the molecular sequences of the DNA
double helix of the cell that random mutation may occur.
It can occur accidentally when DNA is copied in a new
generation. Part of the DNA's double helix may be left out
in the copy. Sometimes a DNA element can insert itself
at a new position in the genome (that is, the entire DNA
map of the species). Yet, such random DNA events--your
molecular biologists have discovered--do not occur fre-
quently or in any automatic way. Rather, the copying of a
mistake in the DNA occurs only once in a generation for
every hundred million of the DNA nucleotides, with rare
exceptions. Within viruses such as HIV and the ever dead-

ly and wicked malaria plasmodium, the mutation rate is much speedier.

But here is the significant observation: few mutations are helpful mutations. As one of my successors wrote recently: it is easier for such micro-evolution to break things than to make things. The tendency is not toward beneficial change but toward autodestruction of the organism, as the information transmission system internal to the cell produces more and more errors. This we now observe empirically. As a biochemical occurrence triggering species change, random mutation is a vandal, a havoc wreaker, thwarting and stopping the cell's interoperating mechanisms. Random mutation as the mechanism of evolutionary change is thus incoherent. It cannot build the cell's integrated molecular systems.

Here is exactly why. Late in your century, your mathematicians demonstrated that unguided trial and error--the correlative of my unguided, chance selection by nature of beneficial mutations--that the principle fails. Without the guidance of algorithms, trial and error (or chance) can solve no problem beyond the most trivial. Every one of your mathematicians, your engineers, your space scientists, your marvelous computer and software technologists knows no role for random chance in the designing and functioning of your fantastic technology. But how much more complex are nature's organisms and their inbuilt genetic programs. For your space shuttles and "Apple" marvels, chance is a non-word. But how do living organisms, so much more complex than any machine assembly of the 21st century, then defy the laws of chance?

What are the chances for change, your mathematicians have asked, when a random mutation takes place in the DNA of an existing organism? Chance, for example, as the agent in the building of novel genes or proteins? Or the exponential number of combinations of amino acids? Mathematics tells biology in your time that even a relatively "short" functional protein made up of a 150-amino acid sequence would constitute one sequence in a chance lottery of other possible sequence combinations that would be astronomically large. I am no specialist in the powers of 10, but I read that the odds for the chance evolution by random mutation of such a living entity as integratedly complex as a short protein exceeds the number of atoms physicists calculate to exist in the entire universe. Your famous cosmologist Hoyle calculated the odds of producing the proteins necessary for a simple one-celled organism by chance at a number in powers of 10 absolutely beyond comprehension--in short, byond the reach of chance.

I discover that some have come to speculate on the existence of unknown built-in evolutionary laws yet undiscovered, in order to explain the general evolution of life argued in my Theory. But if there were such laws, and laws are by definition non-random. such laws would have to have had the designs we see in all species--already written in!

As I learned and meditated on all of this, there emerged in my mind the critical question about the cell, about my general Idea, and about me. How could even the simplest cell, vast in complexity, have then suddenly assembled itself? The utter and total unalterable interdependence of the cell's subsystems is *all*. When I learned of the cell's--every cell's--fantastic structures, labyrinths, circuits, gateways, all complete with a built-in blueprint and translation, communication and even self-replication mechanisms, I was struck in the most powerful way by the *fitting together* of all the complete parts, the infinitesimal, interdependent molecular machines that make up the cell's mechanized factory. And the amazingly diverse cells of the living world have no ancestors--they have programs. Indeed, the very concept of "primitive," primordial, ancestor cells is an absurdity.

And so I again ask myself: how could such a factory assemble itself, consonant with my Idea? The factory-cell functions, based on the information that its internal DNA double helix transmits within it. But here is a further question your scientists have raised: the double helix is only a data storage bank and transmitter for information. Information itself has no physical attribute or dimension, no atoms or molecules. How does the double helix and its fantastically specified molecules get the information it codes and acts on? Have your biologists not now discovered that something nonmaterial, nonorganic actuates and drives the living world? The DNA molecule is matter, but the information it holds is not matter. It is nonmaterial. It is a different domain than matter. Biology has an immaterial component--information--in the cells of every living thing on earth.

That component is just as real and actual as anything physical or material. With us, information originates in our processing of our sensory data into thoughts, which

have no physical, material dimension. We create information, and yet we now know in your time that information
is found in biology, which we did not create. I ask: where
did the information coded in the cell's DNA come from?
How can a thing that has no physical organic reality origi-
nate, evolve--as I declared all life to have evolved from
what I believed was a primordial single cell--across life's
great divisions through genera, orders, classes to phyla?
As one of your scientists has lately said: the DNA molecule is the medium, but it is not the message.

Is it not now dawning on us at the 150th anniversary
of the fabled "revolution" that bears my name, that the information which directs every living cell has to have preceded the physical material structure of the double helix,
RNA, and protein molecules?

From the subcellular to the species--what a biochemical mountain to climb! The assembly of functionally specified molecules, the forming of them into multimolecular
systems which are combined into the uniting of diverse
types of cells to form organs. Organ systems brought together into the complete organism. Here are the building blocks of a living thing--a species, an organic system
whose subsystems are coadapted to interact functionally.

When I imagine the biochemical mountain that must
be climbed to reach the grail of a species at the mountain's
peak, I must now imagine nature's climb as vastly multiple. There is not one climber, but many. They hack out
separate paths of ascent, yet they must do so together in
time, somehow collaboratively, for they must constantly
co-adapt one to another. The climbers must separately

climb, and the subsystems must separately evolve, but in a miraculous lockstep, for they must all reach the peak simultaneously in order to emerge as an immensely complex interdependent, integrated whole. How? Not explained. I am appalled by the "just so" stories to which some of my successors resort.

A brilliant molecular biologist of your time, Behe, has drawn an irrefutable conclusion. Nature presents us with the incontestible fact of cellular structures that are irreducibly complex--the bacterial flagellar motor with its 30-part biochemical rotary engine, for example. The component parts of such structures interact functionally in a complex intricacy such that the mutational alteration of one component stops the mechanism, renders it inoperable, just as the insertion of a mal-sized cog in a clockworks stops the clock. This fundamental and irrefutable fact of molecular biological reality became well known by the late 1980s, over twenty years ago.

The cell, which carries both the instructions and the mechanisms to build its functional self and is only an element of an unimaginably more complex organ, collapses my Theory's information-free, thought-free, plan-free central principle. Complexity defies chance, complexity specified by its own actuating information eliminates chance. Complexity that is irreducible, that cannot function in the absence of a single one of its interoperable parts, compels me to recognize that your age has empirically established a biological reality incompatible with my general Theory and of the greatest scientific import.

And here, I take note of further revolutionary discoveries in your time in realms of science beyond my ken. I discovered that a general consensus now exists among your astrophysicists that our universe is indeed "fine tuned" for life on our planet. That is a conclusion of the most profound consequence. As one of them has said, our universe is a cosmos and not a chaos. Was it not your famous physicist Einstein, who revolutionized the world's understanding of cosmic time and of matter, who said that God did not "play dice with the universe"?

I believed firmly that nature played dice, that natural, chance selection acting on random mutations fully and totally explained the origin and descent of the living world. Your discovery of the molecular basis of life revealed with absolute finality that nature too is fine-tuned. If science is to remain honest (as some of your Soviet scientists, I read, were not), if we are to pursue truth wherever it leads, the fine-tuning of the natural world too can no longer be disputed. Could life exist without the *fitness*--for our carbon-based life--of water, the light, the elements, carbon, the metals, the cell, the vital gases, the double helix?

And now I, whom history made tribune of the unguided evolution of all life forms, am compelled to accept the empirical evidence of molecular nature's built-in constraints on evolutionary change. Evolution within the species barrier is evident, that is, micro-evolutionary change. Beyond that barrier, perhaps we have a definitional problem. The edge of evolution is very small. It does not encompass the great phyla of nature.

Something else must explain the intricacy present in all life's astonishing diversity. Something else must account for the Cambrian Explosion. Something else must explain the fact that the nonmaterial information, which is coded and conveyed by life's DNA structure to its subcellular protein factories, had to be there *before* the body plans of today's vertebrate life, which appeared so suddenly in geological time.

Organized information is that something, information to design and program every molecular detail and function of every species in the great plenitude of earth's life. Organized information requires precedent intelligence, organized and programmed information on the absolute order of magnitude I have described. And it necessitates an omniscient intelligence, a single, unique, timeless force of being preceding the universe of order which that force set in motion in the Big Bang cosmos.

So I must conclude that information-based life on earth from its ancient beginnings was intelligence-guided, designed by an omniscient intelligence in the vastness of cosmic time to culminate in the unique apprehending, thinking, reasoning, creating species that we are, a species compelled by the empirical evidence in cosmos and microcosm to recognize an originating, guiding, creative intelligence beyond all stars before all worlds, author and guide of the expanding universe and the unfolding history of life on our planet.

Why have those incontrovertible facts of cosmic and natural reality not overwhelmed you with wonder, awe, humility? Everywhere, the integrated complexity of the fine-tuned laws of nature, the properties of matter, the details of the living world, the events of the cosmos, point incontestably to a precisioned physical reality of intelligent design.

Do you not grasp that you confront, in your time, *infinities*? Not only the infinity of the cosmos and of the atom and subatomic, but the infinity of the biological world?

VIII

THE TURNING

*I look with confidence to the future, to young and rising
naturalists, who will be able to view both sides of the
question with impartiality.*

C.D.

*The transfer of allegiance from paradigm to paradigm
is a conversion experience that cannot be forced. . . .The
source of resistance is the assurance that the older paradigm will ultimately solve all its problems, that nature
can be shoved into the box the paradigm provides.*

Thomas Kuhn

AND SO MY fabulous errand, my return to the millen-
nial new world of 2009, comes to an end. As I depart to
whence I came, I will leave you with these humble observations.

I knew when I spoke my last words at Down House
to my dear Emma that my Idea had transformed science
and had given the world a new and revolutionary picture
of human reality. In my time with you, I have studied the
paradoxical evolution and devolution of my Theory, and I
have measured the powerful impact of my Theory on the
social and political world of the violent and astonishing
century that followed my own. Through the intensest of
inquiries--for my eye is as bright now as it was aboard the
Beagle--I have observed many things.

My Idea, more than any other, lies at the heart of your
fundamental confusion about human reality in this first
decade of the 21st century. That Idea, which convinced the
world that the saga of life flowed from an original cosmic
accident through a vast blind mechanism to the infinite
capacity of the brain of Einstein--that Idea was my own.
My Theory robbed man of that which set him apart from
all other creatures. It reduced him to a plaything of the col-

lectivist secular creeds of your time so lethal of historical consequence. My Idea stamped the seal of science on the concept of man as malleable, perfectible higher hominid, maker of his own identity, morality, destiny.

I have observed the ineluctible falling away of my Idea before the stunning testimony of an emergent new science now taking its place on the far, far side of complexity.

I was indeed aware that my grand edifice was entirely theoretical. Yet it changed the world. You speak of the "Darwinian Revolution," just as you honor equally the Newtonian, the Copernican revolutions. You write and teach of the "materialist paradigm" that my Idea fixed in the modern mind. You made of me, legend, alpha and omega prophet of a sovereign blind and mindless Nature.

One of the more imaginative of my disciples in your time has indeed posed the emergence of a "consilience", based upon my Idea. All human activity, all branches of learning, all social life, by the late 20th century, affirmed and reflected the grand role I outlined for the random unguided play of chance effects upon natural laws. My Theory of Everything! One of your historians has pronounced it "the greatest idea ever." With "consilience," I became dogma, *Origin* and *Descent* annexed as texts of a Church of Darwin. There are mountains named for me, species of life, academic sinecures, even a city in Australia, commemoration days.

I had not expected an evolution of Evolution into a belief system! That my Idea in the century to come would petrify into unassailable dogma, a mataphysics hostile to dissent, to heretical ideas, guarded about by custodians of the secrets like the ancient Egyptian priests--I had not foreseen.

The conversion of the mind of man to my Theory and its author congealed in your time into a closed evolutionary school hostile to counter-inquiry, dismissive of criticism, and blind to contradictory evidence. My champions became negators of science, jailors of mind. My Theory became creed--the Great Myth of the 20th Century. How remarkable it is that the physicists of your time escaped the paradigm clamp that the prophets of materialism, myself included, put in place. The philosophical and religious implications of the Big Bang universe they detected and measured empirically did not trouble them. Why are the physicists of your time free in spirit, but not the biologists?

The believer-disciple of whom I just spoke had it quite backwards. The great discoveries the world has seen in your century and time--in molecular biology, in the astonishing, fine balance of the chemistry of the earth, in the fossils' unexpected testimony, in the revelations of your astrophysicists--all these conjoin in an empirical denial of a universe and a living world formed from a random, unguided playing out of unintelligent matter. You are witnessing consilience, but it is an evidential consilience of something you and I did not expect.

Let us first acknowledge that the inquirers among your molecular biologists have put in place a fact as incontestible as that the earth orbits the sun. Between the organic and the inorganic worlds, between the simplest living form and lifeless matter, the chasm is unbridgeable. Not only are there no transitional states of matter nonliving and living, such entities are, let us say, conceptually, molecularly impossible.

My competence was the living world--its origins and processes and its fossilized evidence. My Idea has been the world's dynamic idea for 150 years, shaping decisively the modern mind, science's seal to the notion of an un-Godded universe. The reign of my Idea is now ending. My assertion of the blind evolution of life from a single cell to the infinite ranges of the biochemical-electrical synapse circuitry of the human brain falls before the overwhelming evidence of information-based, information-actuated processes of life in cell and genome. That information, specified and complex, can have no other origin than in the design of a great creative intelligence beyond human measure.

To reduce design, manifestly evident in all nature, to "appearance of design" as casuists of your time have argued, is as fatuous and sure a signal of cognitive defeat as that the earth orbits around the "appearance of a sun-star." To say that design is accidental is to say that the space station circling the earth in 2009 assembled itself in a storm of cosmic wind. Specified complexity cannot *not* require a designer. Design without precedent intelligence fails the laws of causality and all rationality. Design is the inarguable, fundamental descriptor of the universe and the material, natural world.

Science ineluctibly follows truth where it will lead. Science has now put in place a new/old idea and paradigm of cosmos and life, supplanting my revelation of 1859. The concept of the continuity of all nature has long existed in the mind of man. In the year 2009, it does not exist in the facts of nature. The great chain of evolution is broken. My Theory was like a stream, once mighty in its course, that ran out in the desert sands. It has not led us to science's great sea, the sea of truth.

Metaphysics is not my competence. I leave to others the implications of the revolution in science that you are experiencing. But I must put to you this question: Who--or what--*is* design's intelligence, the crafter of the non-material information that the DNA of life's cells and organisms codes and transmits to organic action?

That intelligence is everywhere empirically demonstrable in our universe of a measurable primordial beginning and fine-tuned balance of physical laws and forces. It is empirically demonstrable in our living world of astounding integrated complexity, an intricacy beyond marvel.

We stand before the reality of a great, all-encompassing Mind, for intelligence *is* mind. We have reached a juncture in the development of science as great as the passing from the Ptolemaic to the Copernican world. Your riven century, a nexus of brilliance and violence, drops the shackles from our eyes, returning mankind to a re-recognition of the purpose of the creature who stands at the apogee of life, a creature sharing physical and DNA commonalities with other chordates, vertebrates, primates, but utterly distinct in the living world for its unique possession of *mind.*

The death of the materialist paradigm frees our eyes again to focus on the great compass of history. History is the remembered, documented record of humanity, encompassing all thought, all experience, all empirical knowledge, all science. History is how we know and all we know.

I recall again my blessed Emma, whose gentle, steadfast remonstrances reminded me that history's revelations are not those of science only. Well before the first birth of science with the Greeks, a great revelation occurred in the world's "axial time," as your philosopher Jaspers described it, that age when an awareness of a force governing man beyond nature put in place codes of moral law and set the foundations of civilizations simultaneously, independently each of the other, in the valleys and vales of the Ancient World. Axial time witnessed a dawning recognition that man was not nature only, but *spirit.*

Historians tell us then of a turning point which followed, an event unique in human history. Your great Russian novelist Pasternak called it the only true revolution that has ever occurred.

That event gave to history, teleology--a time-line rooted in a new view of the world. History was not a circular thing locked to nature's birth-to-death cycle. History, unfolding in linear time, was ever pregnant with meaning. That perception came from the recognition of the historical event that was unique in time: the entry of the Creator-God into human history as the God-man to free mankind from the shackles of nature, an event that set for all earthly time mankind's aim and purpose as a being both of and beyond nature. Other civilizations produced technology, but modern science arose and developed only in *this* civilization. Why? It was Judeo-Christian civilization, based on belief in a rational God, that viewed the universe and world as intelligible and contingent, promoting a seeking and inquiry, observation, experimentation--and discovery.

I leave you with that final observation. My privileged visitation, but for one remaining place, has ended. Before I prepare to depart, I wish to walk again the Sandwalk at Down. I believe I will not be observed by the latter-day tourists. I will doubtless see the passing curious, old scholars, and, I hope, the young--schoolchildren, young students, young questioning minds. It is to the young, the rising generation, that I have penned the epistle of my peregrenations among you, the testimony of my witness to a new scientific reality and a testament to a new, unafraid and open world.

IX

DOWN HOUSE

Polly, the little fox-terrier, loved this walk [the Terrace Walk] too. My father would pace to and fro, and my mother would sometimes sit on the dry chalky bank waiting for him, and be pulled by him up the little steep pitch on the way home.

Henrietta Darwin

I HAVE COME at last to Down, my beloved house in Kent where I lived my happy life with Emma and to which our sweet children came one by one, the delight of my life. When we moved there, still in our youth, I jested I did not want to turn into a "complete Kentish hog." For it was not provincial peace, but quiet that I sought in the village of Downe, to study and experiment in my window and annex laboratories. How I enjoyed my Sandwalk and the Terrace Walk too, along our beautiful valley. I wanted tranquillity, for I was ill much of my life and nursed by you, my dear wife, my greatest blessing, my wise adviser and comforter, whose memory I seek, but to whom my revolutionary Theory brought pain.

You said that my ideas seemed to you to "be putting God further and further off." Yes, I know that my Idea foreclosed the hand of God. And I knew, too, to what that great denial ultimately led beyond our Christian belief. Its meaning was: *no purpose!*

You wrote me a letter from the heart, saying "my own dearest" would indulge you. And indeed I did love you deeply. You said that my holding to proof in all things might color my approach to things impossible to prove that might be above our comprehension. You wished for and believed in my patience with you. And you told me, my beloved, you should be most unhappy if you thought we did not belong to each other forever.

Did you know of, did you read, the note I inscribed at the end of your letter, my dear Emma?

"When I am dead, know that many times I have kissed and cryed over this. C.D."

And to another letter you wrote I appended this note:

"God bless you."

As I visit old Down again, I consider the charge I have been given. In this testament, I have observed as closely as I know how what became the vast legacy of my Idea and its quixotic impact on the historical world. That was my charge. About my living genetic progeny, I was forbidden contact. You may not interfere in the lives of your grandchildren, which now number in the many generations. This, the Authority instructed.

How I loved to play with my own dear children. On my rounds along the Sandwalk, they would beckon to me to come play. All my life I remembered my little son at four, who tried to bribe me with a sixpence to come and play. And did I not give in, overrule my ever ready compulsion not to waste time?

But I wonder as I walk now the familiar grounds of Down and as I enter, invisibly with the tourists, the sanc-

tum of my study to see the great board on which I wrote
and the couch where a sick child might lie dozing or
watching me as I worked, I wonder and wish with all my
heart to know of my now perhaps four or five generations
of grandchildren and what they all came to do.

Did they marry, did they find happiness like mine?
What did they experience in your terrible time of civilization's great World Wars, which decimated generations of
English boys? Were my grandsons among them, the boys
who fell with so many other English, French, and German
boys on the Marne and at Verdun? My granddaughters-
-were they, with their babies, to be young widows weep-
ing upon telegraphed news from the bloody warfronts of
Europe and the world? That world of posterity of which I
was an instrument in the making? But I was instructed not
to inquire of them. It will not do you any good, I was told.
it is not your commission. But, *O !!*

How I would love an hour with you, my grandchildren in generations now living, to tell you what I have
learned that it might free you as you grow from that great
myth that paralyzed the human spirit in your time. How
I would like to sit with you, hug you, talk to you, tell you
how much I love you, my grandchildren so far removed,
just as I did in those happiest days of my life on earth with
my own precious children.

Along my Sandwalk I see a young boy about eleven
and his little sister, perhaps seven. They walk at not quite
mid-distance before me, my ear sometimes catching their
innocent chatter. I hear by accent they are American. But
do they now sense my too close observation of them, for

both turn now to look at me. I am suddenly not invisible, and I am my old self, dressed as I was then. I feel for my great white beard--yes!

My grandchildren look at me in wonder, their beautiful eyes, the boy's green, the girl's dark brown. But they are unafraid. They recognize me, and there is love in their eyes. My grandchildren!

I close my testament, the report of my errand to earth in my anniversary year, with a question to my grandchildren and to the posterity of my grand Idea of the material origin and nature of all things. What is the origin and descent of love--beyond all the tendentious anthropology, the feeble and contradictory evolutionary psychology of your disbelieving time?

No, we do not possess a "selfish gene" fitting us out to act altruistically for the survival and progress of the race. Would not such a gene compel us to love only the strongest of our offspring, to practice infanticide upon the weakest? But I see that your selfish-gene advocates, bold casuists that they are, emphasize that it is not the gene itself but only its *effects* that make the gene *appear* selfish!

And so I no longer say that my dear Emma's love, my children's love and my love for them, I no longer declare that it emerged out of cosmic/microcosmic accident. How gladly would I have given my life for little Annie my daughter so sweet of face, coquettish as she turned along the Sandwalk to delight me in some way from her bright nature, and when, at ten years of age, she was dying, for as we nursed her, we could not save her, the love she gave us in her eyes and in her last word was an utterly selfless love: "I quite thank you."

O, how I loved her, my sweet little daughter brought into this world by my dearest Emma. Why must I have loved her so? Where is the gene, the molecular strand in me that possesses, translates, enables the message of the love which I have felt to its very furthest depths, this immaterial thing that is at the center of my being? The gene strand for my love is not there, is not in the DNA which I in my time unbeknownst possessed. Where did it come from?

Give me your answer, my anniversary celebrants who embarass me exceedingly with "Darwin Day." Where is the gene that does not exist that would make me say to deaf heaven, or to God?: *Take me! Take me, not her!*

I am again on my beloved Sandwalk with the children. Are they truly my very own posterity, these children of 2009 who look at me so lovingly, as if I am indeed their old grandfather of a distant generation? Yes, they know me! I break my promise--or is my promise being broken for me? The boy and the girl run to my open arms. I embrace them, hug them, kiss them. They are my own! What are your names, I ask?

Andrew!

Alison!

I place my testament in their young hands.

Goodbye, I say. I love you, I love you.

PERSONAE

Persons Noted in Mr. Darwin's Journal

THE BRIEF BIOGRAPHICAL notes appended here are provided to identify for readers some 45 figures Mr. Darwin has mentioned in the journal of his unannounced visitation to earth in the bicentennial year of his birth and the sesquicentennial of *The Origin of Species*. Included are not only past and contemporary figures key to Darwin's scientific interests and inquiries. Also identified are philosophers, historians, writers, and political and literary figures whose shaping influence on, and action roles in, the crisis of 20th and early 21st century civilization likewise attracted his doggedly inquiring observational powers.

Louis Agassiz (d. 1873). Agassiz was a Swiss-American zoologist and geologist well known during and beyond Darwin's time for his fossil studies and prominent exposition of glacial movement. A dissenting correspondent of Darwin's who, unlike many contemporary associates, did not adopt evolution's anti-religious implications.

Aristotle (384-322 B.C.). A founding figure in Western philosophy and science, Aristotle introduced into the mind of Ancient Greece and posterity the notion of an all-embracing materialism, incorporating all form, growth, motion, and change.

Michael Behe (b. 1952). Lehigh University molecular biologist whose widely influential *Darwin's Black Box: The Biochemical Challenge to Evolution* (1996) foreclosed evolution by neo-Darwinian natural selection of the interoperating, interdependent, intricate and complex molecular structures of the cell such as the irreducibly complex bacterial flagellum, for which design remains the only plausible explanation. Behe's *Edge of Evolution* (2007) limits the possibility of evolution by natural selection acting on random mutations to small changes.

Auguste Comte (d. 1857). French founder of Positivism, a philosophical system based wholly on modern positive sciences, foremost, sociology, a term of his own invention. Laid out in *Course of Positive Philosophy* (1830-1842), Comptean positivism was a prime mover in the spread of secular views of the world and social reality in Darwin's time and later.

Robert Conquest (b. 1917). Eminent British historian, writer, and scholar at the London School of Economics, Columbia University, the Woodrow Wilson Center, and the Hoover Institution of War, Revolution, and Peace. His historical works, *The Great Terror* (1968) and *Harvest of Sorrow* (1986), provided a solid documented record of Stalin's purges in the Soviet terror state and the Communist forced famine in the Ukraine. Conquest's *Reflections on a Ravaged Century* (2000) underscored the perverse and distorted "mindslaughter" central to the great 20th-century ideologies of revolutionary Marxism and National Socialism.

Nicholas Copernicus (1473-1543). The Polish astronomer whose observations, advanced in his treatise *De revolutionibus orbium coelestium* (1543), described convincingly a sun-centered planetary system and thus a no longer earth-centered universe. The Copernican Revolution vastly extended intellectual horizons and established the basis of modern astronomy and astrophysics.

Emma Wedgwood Darwin (d. 1896). Darwin married his first cousin, daughter of the famous potter Josiah Wedgwood, in 1839, three years after returning to England from his voyage. Together they had ten children, seven of whom lived to adulthood. Darwin's autobiographical sketch reflects a happy marriage and devoted family life in the village of Downe, Kent, where they lived from 1842 on. Emma did needlework and was an archer and rode horses. She danced and skated, read German, French, and Italian, and played the piano. Darwin played backgammon with her evenings and liked to hear her play Beethoven and Handel.

Henrietta Darwin (Litchfield) (d. 1929). Darwin's daughter Henrietta threw light on family life at Down House in editing and publishing *Emma Darwin, A Century of Family Letters* (1904).

Richard Dawkins (b. 1941). The well-known British evolutionary biologist is perhaps the foremost living spokesman for neo-Darwinism (*The Selfish Gene*, 1976 and *The Blind Watchmaker*, 1986), as well as a militant defender and promoter of atheism (*The God Delusion*, 2006) and outspoken critic of the legitimacy of biological research conflicting with Darwinian premises and conclusions. His notion of "selfish genes" postulates that genetically related individuals will tend to behave selflessly, which for the materialist Dawkins explains altruistic human feelings and actions. From that premise, he further speculates on deterministic "memes"--evolutionary cultural equivalents to genes--an inventive, documentarily absurd extension of biological evolution into the free realm of human action in history.

Michael Denton (b. 1952). A British-Australian biologist educated at Kings College, London, whose influential *Evolution: A Theory in Crisis* (1985) summarized late-century scientific developments refuting Darwin's gradualist model, including the failure of homology, the noncorroboration of the fossil record, and the molecular biological revolution. His *Nature's Destiny: How the Laws of Biology Reveal Purpose in the Universe* (1998) emphasized the uncanny *fitness*, both of the physical laws of the universe and the biochemistry and environment of the earth to host and maintain life through the "long chain of coincidences" that gave mankind its terrestial home.

John Dewey (d. 1952). Pragmatist philosopher and probably the most influential American educator of the early 20th century (*Democracy and Education*, 1916). Dewey was a philosophical progressive who regarded truth to be not fixed and eternal but evolutionary, placing education for citizenship above strict intellectual attainment.

Albert Einstein (d. 1955). The father of modern physics and Nobel laureate whose fundamental scientific contributions--the special and general theories of relativity, mass-energy equivalence, photon theory, wave-particle

duality, and the quantum theory of atomic motion in sol-
ids--made him a towering figure in 20th century science.
General relativity established the basis of cosmological
models of the expanding universe.

Ludwig Feuerbach (d. 1872). In *Das Wesen des
Christentums* (1841), the German philosopher declared that
nothing existed outside man and nature and that God was
the projection of man's thoughts and ideals. God was the
creation of man. Though more a humanist than a materialist, he greatly influenced subsequent materialist thinking,
asserting that religion was but a symbolic "dream."

Captain Robert FitzRoy (d. 1865). British Naval officer
FitzRoy was captain of H.M.S. *Beagle* during the survey
and research voyage of 1831-1836 for which he selected
Darwin as a research companion. FitzRoy later served as
governor of New Zealand, was subsequently elected to the
Royal Society, and was prominent in development of naval meteorological technology. He attained Vice-Admiral
grade in late life.

Sigmund Freud (d. 1939). The founder of psychoanal-
ysis and theoretician of human social and cultural behavior whose great impact on modern thought included not
only psychology, anthropology, education, and art and
literature, but popular moral notions of human behavior
and relationships. More than any other thinker, Freud's
assertion of the primacy of subconscious drives over the
rational mind influenced individual moral behavior in the
20th century.

Francis Galton (d. 1911). The English polymath Galton
was a cousin of Darwin, profoundly influenced by *Origin*

of Species. He was a pioneer in several scientific fields, including meteorology and statistical measurement. Using the latter tool, he undertook extensive research focused on variations in human classes and populations, inventing the term *eugenics* in 1883. He early suggested the sterilization of social "undesirables," a concept that, in the early 20th century, grew to include the physically and mentally handicapped. Galton inspired the founding in England of the Eugenics Education Society in 1907.

Stephen Jay Gould (d. 2002). Harvard paleontologist and evolutionary biologist Gould's signal idea and challenge to Darwinian gradualism was his theory of "punctuated equilibrium." Long periods of evolutionary stability were broken by sudden change. His influential *Ontogeny and Phylogeny* was complimented by many popularly written books, including *The Panda's Thumb* and *Wonderful Life*, and he wrote and appeared in many fora and venues.

Ernst Haeckel (d. 1919). Haeckel was Darwin's primary German disciple and enthusiastic publicist. Darwin relied on the German biologist's doctored drawings of exaggerated, idealized, and inaccurate vertebrate embryos to support common descent, as do many biology textbooks to this day, despite evolutionary biologist Stephen Jay Gould's characterization of the faked drawings as "scientific fraud." Haeckel's immensely popular writings also greatly contributed to late-19th and early-20th century attitudes of biological racism and inspired evolutionary ethics and eugenics theory and practices. His *The Natural History of Creation* (1868) depicted a "descending" order of facial profiles, European through black African

and Tasmanian to species of apes. It stated that "the differences between the lowest humans and the highest apes
are smaller than the differences between the lowest and
the highest humans." By devaluing "primitive" races, his
writings acted to encourage a later genocidal mentality.

Adolf Hitler (d. 1945). No figure in modern history
personifies more the composite evil of absolute state power and lethal racial ideology unrestrained by a traditional
moral code. Hitler presided over the Nazi genocide-demo-
cide state that in its concentration and death camps and
other lethal venues murdered, separate from military action, almost 21 million people, of which almost 6 million
European Jews and over 10 million Slavs were the large
fractions.

Fred Hoyle (d. 2001). Cambridge astronomer whose
study of the structure of stars and the origin of chemi-
cal elements in stars led him to conclude that the earth's
carbon-based life must have required a "super-calculating
intellect" in order to have assembled the properties of
the carbon atom. He held that its creation by blind physical forces was statistically "miniscule," a conclusion that
moved him to postulate a guiding force in the universe.
Hoyle proposed that earth's life arose elsewhere in the
universe and was "seeded" on earth by comets ("pansper-
mia"). Proponent of steady-state theory, he rejected on
philosophical grounds the subsequently established Big
Bang origin of the universe.

Julian Huxley (d. 1975). English evolutionary biologist and grandson of Darwin's famous defender Thomas
Huxley, he played a major role in assembly of the neo-Dar-

winian synthesis through his best-known work, *Evolution: the Modern Synthesis* (1942). He also wrote *Evolution in Action* (1953) and many other books. An advocate of secular humanism, he was also a president of the British Eugenics Society.

Thomas H. Huxley (d. 1895). Darwin's biologist-friend, major English disciple, and popular, militant proponent and publicist of Darwinian evolutionary theory, for which he received the appellation "Darwin's Bulldog." Though possessing little formal education, the autodidact Huxley acquired standing in comparative anatomy. Author of *Evidence of Man's Place in Nature* (1863), he also publicized a claim for *Archaeopteryx* as the missing link between putative reptile-to-bird evolution, a major factor in popular acceptance of Darwinian theory, but a claim now rejected by most paleontologists as the ancestor of modern birds.

Karl Jaspers (d. 1969). The German philosopher and Heidelberg professor described the period 800-200 B.C. as history's "axial age", when, in a "quantum leap," universal concepts of religion and philosophy emerged independently and simultaneously in the Middle East (Judaism), Greece (classical philosophy), India (Buddhism, Hinduism), and China (Confucianism, Taoism), each producing Natural Law moral codes including variations on a Golden Rule.

Thomas S. Kuhn (d. 1996). The historian and philosopher of science and author of the widely influential *The Structure of Scientific Revolutions* (1962) documented major revolutions in science which have led to paradigm shifts, each of great moment in the establishment of a new, prevailing scientific view. Kuhn's study presents an anatomy of the pattern and discusses the impact of major scientists like Lavoisier, Priestley, and Franklin, while placing most emphasis on the revolutions set in motion by Copernicus, Newton, and Einstein. Kuhn's insights bear on both the Darwinian revolution and paradigm (to which, however, he oddly devotes little attention), and on the current challenge to that paradigm by a rising generation of intelligent-design molecular biologists and mathematicians.

Jean Baptiste Lamarck (d. 1829). Lamarck, a French naturalist who introduced evolutionary ideas, formulated the theory of inheritance of acquired characteristics, which Darwin adopted. Lamarck's theory gave way in early 20th-century Darwinian theory to Mendel's laws of genetic inheritance.

Louis and Mary Leakey (d. 1972, d. 1996). The patriarchal couple of the family famous in paleoanthropological work in East Africa. Mary Leakey's 1960 discovery of human-like skull fragments in the Olduvai Gorge in Tanzania, together with primitive tool finds, led to the Leakeys' claim to the earliest member of the genus *Homo*, *Homo habilis* ("handyman") dated at 2 million years antiquity. Professional and personal disputes between the Leakeys and with other researchers characterized the subsequent contentious science of paleoanthropology. Discovery of "Lucy", hominid fossil remains purported to be at 3.2 million years, the "grandmother of humanity" unearthed in Ethiopia in 1974, overturned the Leakey claims but has been supplanted in turn by later candidates such as *Orrorin tugenesis* in Kenya, dated to 6 million years ago.

Vladimir (Ilyich) Lenin (d. 1924). The prime actor in the Bolshevik seizure of power in 1917 and founder of Soviet Russia and the international Comintern made revolutionary Communism the dominant political fact of most of the war- and revolution-torn 20th century. He created the Soviet terror-state, which by policy and practice killed almost 62 million designated "enemies of the state" in the ensuing four decades and beyond.

Thomas Malthus (d. 1834). Malthus's thesis that human populations would always increase to exceed supporting resources, published as *An Essay on the Principle of Population* (1798), failed to foresee man's capacity to increase food and other resources, while it also parented future "population bomb" forecasts. Darwin adapted to his own Theory the Malthus notion that, in the competition for resources, the fittest would survive.

Mao Zedong (d. 1976). The revolutionary father of Chinese Communism and first dictator of the People's Republic of China, whose purges, collectivization killings, and radical social programs--the Great Leap Forward (1957-1960) and Cultural Revolution (1965-1968)--resulted in the deaths of over 35 million Chinese men, women, and children.

Karl Marx (d. 1883). The German revolutionary and, with Friedrich Engels, founder of Communism (*The Communist Manifesto*, 1848) and foremost theoretician of modern socialism (*Das Kapital*, 1867). Marx's proposition that social revolution to eliminate free market capitalism was necessary to the attainment of universal equality laid the basis for future socialist theory and practice, both democratic socialism and the establishment of socialist/ communist regimes by violent revolution.

Gregor Mendel (d. 1884). Moravian monk and scientist whose systematic botanical experimentation with garden peas led to the discovery that transmission of characteristics from parent to subsequent generations was governed by genetic "factors", which were later termed genes. Mendel's laws of genetic inheritance, little known until rediscovered in 1900 by Hugo de Vries and others, refuted Darwin's Lamarckian notion of transmission of parental acquired characteristics.

Sir Isaac Newton (1642-1727). The great English physicist and philosopher who formulated the law of gravitation and the laws of motion.

Friedrich Nietzsche (d. 1900). Nietzsche's condemnation of Christian morality as the slave morality of the masses in *Thus Spake Zarathustra* and other writings emphasized the emergence of the morally superior overman (*Uebermensch*) beyond good and evil, the destroyer of the decadent democratic order. His assault on the values and moral virtues of Western Civilization was far-reaching, and the appeal of morally-free Nietzschean man endures to this day despite its inspiration to a new 20th-century human type: totalitarian monsters.

Boris Pasternak (d. 1960). The Russian poet and novelist was awarded the Nobel Prize for Literature in 1958. His novel, *Doctor Zhivago* (1957), contributed to the Soviet dissident movement and reasserted Christian Orthodox elements in the long censored literature of the officially atheist Soviet regime.

Ptolemy (d. 151 (?) A.D.). The Greco-Egyptian astronomer and mathematician through whose *Almagest* was established the long dominant view of the cosmos, regnant until overturned in the 16th century, by Copernicus. The Ptolemaic universe placed the earth at its stationary center, around which all the heavenly bodies revolved.

Pol Pot (Saloth Sar) (d. 1998). Paris-schooled radical socialist revolutionary whose Khmer Rouge movement seized power in Cambodia upon the strategic defeat of America in neighboring Vietnam in 1975. Seeking to establish a Communist utopia through root and branch destruction of society, Pol Pot presided over the Cambodian Holocaust of 1975-1979 in which approximately one-quarter of the population were forcibly marched from the cities and killed or died from torture, exposure, and starvation in jungle camps.

Michael Ruse (b. 1940). British-born philosopher of biology and professor at Canadian and American universities, he is an active critic of the burgeoning intelligent design school of biologists, mathematicians, physicists, and others. He has been prominent in the intelligent design - neo-Darwinism debates of recent decades and is the author of many books, including *Darwinism and its Discontents* (2007) and *Philosophy After Darwin (2009)*.

Raymond Sontag (d. 1972). Prominent American diplomatic historian whose historical study *A Broken World:1919-1939* analyzed the political and cultural factors leading to the recession of democracy and the appeal and rise of totalitarianism in the period following the First World War.

Herbert Spencer (d. 1903). The English philosopher Spencer adopted Darwin's evolutionary theory as the unifying principle of knowledge and applied it universally in an influential series of "The Principles of. . ." books on biology, psychology, sociology, and ethics between 1862 and 1891, "survival of the fittest" as his adapted watchword.

Iosif (Dzhugashvili) Stalin (d. 1953). The dictator of the Soviet Union from 1927 to his death embodied the 20th century phenomenon of state-ideology displacement of traditional morality more than did any other mass killer of the modern age. Stalin's legacy included the wholesale extermination of the Russian "kulak" peasantry, the forced famine of the Ukraine, the targeted mass executions of the Great Terror, and the vast and lethal forced labor camps of the Gulag Archipelago. The one-time seminary student who rejected God holds the undisputed title of the greatest democidal killer of the 20th century.

Alfred Russel Wallace (d. 1913). Wallace, an English naturalist, pursued studies of Asiatic and Australian fauna contemporaneously with Darwin. He developed the idea of evolution by natural selection independently, and in 1858 sent Darwin an article for comment, announcing his theory. The event prompted Darwin to hasten the summary of his own more extensive exposition of evolution. Both Wallace's essay and Darwin's *Origin of Species* were published in 1859.

James D. Watson (b. 1928) and **Francis Crick** (d. 2004). The Cambridge physicist research team who in February

1953 proved the double helix structure of the DNA (deoxyribonucleic acid) molecule and thereby unlocked the secret of the cell's complex structure and the functioning of its genetic instructions. The historic Watson and Crick discovery was announced in the British scientific journal *Nature* in April 1953. They were awarded the Nobel Prize in Physiology or Medicine in 1962.

Richard M. Weaver (d. 1963). American Southern historian and political philosopher whose influential work *Ideas Have Consequences* (1948) saw the causes of civilizational decline in deleterious societal idea-choices such as materialism, relativism, scientism, and socialism.

Jonathan Wells (b. 1942). American molecular biologist and advocate of intelligent design theory, Wells published *Icons of Evolution* (2000), a critical documentation of perduring popular myths important in past and current popular and academic acceptance of Darwinian theory, including the falsified Miller-Urey Experiment claiming a spontaneous physical self-creation of earth's first life, Ernst Haeckel's misleadingly-drawn embryos, and finch species oscillation in the Galapagos Islands. He notes and documents the continuing common misuse of such reputed "icons" in current college and high school biology texts.

Mr. Darwin's Select List of Writings Consulted

This list of books and articles, which Mr. Darwin entered in the back pages of his journal, cannot reflect the full extent of the visitor's voracious research and reading during his sojourn. The writings he did choose to make special note of and to list are appended here. They provide his own documentation of the legendary visit. For readers' information, publication data and in some cases subtitles have been added to Darwin's jotted entries. Mr. Darwin's grant of willed invisibility obviously inhibits any attempt to document additionally his apparently global research travels.

Michael J. Behe. *Darwin's Black Box: The Biological Challenge to Evolution.* The Free Press, 1996.

_____. *The Edge of Evolution: The Search for the Limits of Darwinism.* The Free Press, 2007.

Karl Dietrich Bracher. *The Age of Ideologies: A History of Political Thought in the Twentieth Century.* St. Martin's Press, 1982.

Robert Conquest. *The Great Terror: Stalin's Purge of the Thirties.* Macmillan, 1968.

99

_____. *The Harvest of Sorrow: Soviet Collectivization and the Terror Famine.* University of Alberta Press, 1986.

_____. *Stalin, Breaker of Nations.* Viking, 1991.

_____. *Reflections on a Ravaged Century.* W.W. Norton, 2000.

Simon Conway Morris. *The Crucible of Creation: The Burgess Shale and the Rise of Animals* [in the Cambrian Explosion]. Oxford University Press, 1998.

_____. "Darwin's Dilemma: The Realities of the Cambrian Explosion," in *Philosophical Transactions of the Royal Society,* June 2006.

Stephane Courtois et. al. *The Black Book of Communism: Crimes, Terror, Repression.* Harvard University Press, 1999.

Robert Cowley, ed. *The Cold War: A Military History.* Random House, 2005.

Frederick C. Crews, ed. *Unauthorized Freud: Doubters Confront a Legend.* Viking Penguin, 1998.

Richard Dawkins. *The Selfish Gene.* Oxford University Press, 1976.

_____. *The Blind Watchmaker: Why the Evidence Reveals a Universe without Design.* Norton, 1987.

William A. Dembski. *The Design Inference: Eliminating Chance Through Small Probabilities.* Cambridge University Press, 1998.

_____. *The Design Revolution.* InterVarsity Press, 2004.

Michael Denton. *Evolution: A Theory in Crisis.* Adler & Adler, 1986.

_____. *Nature's Destiny: How the Laws of Biology Reveal Purpose in the Universe.* The Free Press, 1998.

Niles Eldredge. *Darwin: Discovering the Tree of Life.* W.W. Norton, 2005.

Niles Eldredge and Stephen J. Gould. "Punctuated Equilibria: An Alternative to Phyletic Gradualism," 1972, in Eldredge, *Time Frames.* Princeton University Press, 1985.

Niall Ferguson. *The War of the World: Twentieth-Century Conflict and the Descent of the West.* Penguin Books, 2006.

Sigmund Freud. *The Basic Writings of Sigmund Freud.* Modern Library/Random House, 1995.

Martin Gilbert. *The First World War: A Complete History.* Henry Holt & Co.,1994.

_____. *The Second World War: A Complete History.* Henry Holt & Co.,1989.

_____. *The Holocaust: A History of the Jews of Europe during the Second World War.* Henry Holt & Co., 1987.

_____. *A History of the Twentieth Century* (3 vol.). William Morrow and Company, 1997, 1998, 1999.

George Gilder. *Microcosm: The Quantum Revolution in Economics and Technology.*   Simon & Schuster, 1989.

Stephen J. Gould. *Ontogeny and Phylogeny.* The Belknap Press of Harvard University Press, 1977.

_____. *The Panda's Thumb.* Norton, 1984.

Guillermo Gonzalez and Jay W. Richards.*The Privileged Planet: How Our Place in the Cosmos Was Designed for Discovery.* Regnery, 2004.

K. Thalia Grant and Gregory B. Estes. *Darwin in Galapagos: Footsteps to a New World.* Princeton University Press, 2009.

Stephen Hawking. *A Brief History of Time: From the Big Bang to Black Holes.* Bantam Books, 1988.

Adolf Hitler. *Mein Kampf* (1925, 1926), English translation, Hurst & Blackett Ltd., 1939; Houghton Mifflin, 2001.

Julian Huxley. *Evolution: The Modern Synthesis.* Allen & Unwin, 1942.

Karl Jaspers. *The Origin and Goal of History.* Yale University Press,1953.

Paul Johnson. *Modern Times: The World from the Twenties to the Nineties.* Harper Collins, 2001.

Phillip E. Johnson. *Darwin on Trial.* Regnery Gateway, 1991.

Ian Kershaw. *Hitler, the Germans, and the Final Solution.* Yale University Press, 2008.

_____. *Hitler, A Biography.* W.W. Norton, 2008.

Thomas S. Kuhn. *The Structure of Scientific Revolutions.* University of Chicago Press, 1996.

John Lukacs. *At the End of an Age.* Yale University Press, 2002.

Gerhard Masur. *Prophets of Yesterday: Studies in European Culture,1890-1914.* Macmillan, 1961.

Stephen C. Meyer. "The Cambrian Information Explosion: Evidence for Intelligent Design," in *Debating Design: From Darwin to DNA,* ed. W. Dembski and M. Ruse. Cambridge University Press, 2004.

_____. *Signature in the Cell.* Harper Collins, 2009.

Reinhold Niebuhr. *The Nature and Destiny of Man* (2 vol.). Nisbet & Company, Ltd., 1941.

Friedrich Nietzsche. *Beyond Good and Evil.* Regnery, n.d.

Boris Pasternak. *Doctor Zhivago.* Pantheon, 1958.

Richard Pipes. *Russia Under the Bolshevik Regime*. Alfred A. Knopf, 1993.

_____. *The Unknown Lenin: From the Secret Archive*. Yale University Press, 1996.

R.J. Rummel. *Death by Government*. Transaction Publishers, 1997.

Igor Shafarevich. *The Socialist Phenomenon*. Harper & Row, 1980.

Phillip Short. *Mao: A Life*. Henry Holt & Co., 2000.

_____. *Pol Pot: Anatomy of a Nightmare*. Henry Holt & Co., 2005.

Aleksandr Solzhenitsyn. *The Gulag Archipelago, 1918-1956* (3 vol.). Harper & Row, 1973, 1974, 1975, 1978.

Raymond Sontag. *A Broken World 1919-1939, The Rise of Modern Europe*. Harper & Row, 1971.

George Sorel. *Reflections on Violence*. Collier Books, 1961.

Benjamin A. Valentino. *Final Solutions: Mass Killing and Genocide in the 20th Century, Cornell Studies in Security Affairs*. Cornell University Press, 2004.

James D. Watson. *Molecular Biology of the Gene*. Benjamin, 1965.

_____. *The Double Helix* (ed. Gunther Stent). Norton, 1980.

James D. Watson and Francis H.C. Crick. "A Structure of Deoxyribonucleic Acid," *Nature* 171 (1953).

Peter Watson. *The Modern Mind: An Intellectual History of the Twentieth Century*. Perennial/Harper Collins, 2001.

Richard Weikart. *From Darwin to Hitler: Evolutionary Ethics, Eugenics, and Racism in Germany*. Palgrave Macmillan, 2004.

Jonathan Weiner. *The Beak of the Finch: A Story of Evolution in Our Time.* Alfred A. Knopf, 1994.

Jonathan Wells. *Icons of Evolution, Science or Myth.* Regnery, 2002.

Alfred North Whitehead. *Science and Philosophy.* Philosophical Library, 1974.

Karl A. Wittfogel. *Oriental Despotism: A Comparative Study of Total Power.* Vintage Books, 1981.

ACKNOWLEDGMENTS

ACKNOWLEDGMENT IS MADE to the many authors of books here consulted and sometimes paraphrased in the writing of Darwin's journal. Their works appear in the appended list of readings above.

Thanks are due to several pioneering studies in the ongoing and historic scientific and intellectual critique of neo-Darwinian evolutionary theory and philosophical naturalism, which Darwin's revolutionary idea was long believed to have sealed in amber forever. In the 21st century, science has established that nature is not all there is, matter is not all that there is after all. Humanity does not inhabit a universe of chaos and a chance-evolved living world, but a terrestial and cosmic reality that empirically bears witness to beginning, order, balance, and design. That advance in scientific understanding--and Charles Darwin's fictional journal in particular--owe especially to the scientific challenge to a once all-encompassing, now moribund, theory of life by early academic critics: Michael Denton, Phillip E. Johnson, Michael J. Behe, William A. Dembski, and Stephen C. Meyer. The crisis and impending collapse of Darwinian based biology and paleontology signalled in their works and those of others point to the approaching end of the long-regnant materialist worldview that so powerfully shaped the history of the 20th century. They signal the emergence of a new paradigm of science and human reality as momentous as the Copernican Revolution, and indeed the Darwinian Revolution of 150 years ago.

A special debt is also due as always to my wife Inge for her love and faithful support.

ABOUT THE AUTHOR

NICKELL JOHN ROMJUE studied European history and German literature at the universities of Missouri, California, and Heidelberg. He is the author of official published studies of the historic doctrinal and institutional reforms and modernization carried through by the United States Army following the Vietnam War, including *From Active Defense to AirLand Battle, The Army of Excellence,* and *American Army Doctrine for the Post-Cold War.* His books are widely used in military education and in many current national stragegic and military studies. His history-themed short stories, collected in *Out of the Riven Century* and *The Black Box - Darwin, Marx, Nietzsche, Freud ,* dramatize *the great why* of the unprecedentedly violent, democidal 20th century. He is the author of a novel of post-World War II life in a small Midwestern town, *Merry Town, Missouri,* and a collection of strange and humorous tales, *Witches of Devon.* He lives with his wife in York County, Virginia.

9 781604 946451